1 3 5 7 9 10 8 6 4 2

Copyright © Sarah Garland 1994

Sarah Garland has asserted her right under the Copyright,
Designs and Patents Act, 1988 to be identified
as the author and illustrator of this work

First published in the United Kingdom 1994
by The Bodley Head Children's Books
Random House, 20 Vauxhall Bridge Road
London, SW1V 2SA

Random House UK Limited Reg. No. 954009

A CIP catalogue record for this book is available
from the British Library

ISBN 0370 31848 X

Printed in China

DOING
CHRISTMAS
Sarah Garland

THE BODLEY HEAD
London

Granny is coming for Christmas.

We will do the shopping,

and boil the pudding,

and dig up the tree,

and get everything ready for Christmas.

It is Christmas Day and here comes Granny.

She is early.

She has brought some presents.

Granny tells stories

until lunchtime.

Then we walk to the park.

It is time to say goodbye.

It is the end of Christmas Day.